BILLY
and the
B·A·B·Y

Tony Bradman
ILLUSTRATED BY JAN LEWIS

PictureLions
An Imprint of HarperCollins*Publishers*

For Nicole and Leanne
T B

First published by HarperCollins in Picture Lions 1992
10 9 8 7 6 5 4 3 2
Copyright © text Tony Bradman 1992
Copyright © illustrations Jan Lewis 1992

ISBN 0 00 664235 7 (PB)

A CIP catalogue record for this book
is available from the British Library.
The Author asserts the moral right to
be identified as the author of this work.

Printed and bound in Hong Kong

This book is set in Educational New Century School Book

Billy's mum was having a baby.

"It's growing inside me," she said. "Just like you did, Billy."

So that's why she's such a funny shape these days, he thought.

Mum asked him if he wanted to feel the baby kick inside her tummy. Billy said he didn't mind.

"Can I have that box?" he said. Mum gave it to him.

Nice, flat, comfortable shoes

Later, Billy was busy in his room. Dad knocked on the door.

"I've got something to show you," he said. "We took lots of pictures when you were a baby."

Billy wasn't all that interested, but he looked at the album to keep Dad happy.

"Can I have a picture?" asked Billy. Dad gave him one.

The next day Billy was drawing a picture, but Mum interrupted him.

"Would you like to see some of your old baby clothes?" she said. "Some might fit the new baby."

The clothes looked very small. They were all right for a baby, but Billy was glad he didn't have to wear things like that any more.

"Can I have this?" he asked. Mum said he could.

A few days later, Billy was looking in his box when Dad called to him. Billy sighed.

"Come and see what I've found," he said. "All your old baby toys."

Dad got them out and played with them. Dads and babies might like them, but Billy didn't think they looked very exciting.

"Can I have this rattle?" he asked. Dad said he could.

At the weekend, Billy wanted to stick something on his box. But Mum said they had to go to the bookshop instead.

They bought lots of books... and all of them were about babies. Some of them were quite interesting. But most of them weren't.

"Can I have this one for my box?" he asked. It was
an old book, one of his favourites. Mum said he could.

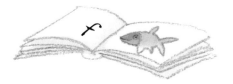

One afternoon, Dad said they had to go out. Billy wanted to work on his box, but he didn't make a fuss.

They went to the hospital where Mum was going to have the baby. They had a look round, and then they had to wait for a long time. It was very warm, and Dad dozed off.

"Can I have that?" asked Billy when they got home. Dad said he could.

Billy had nearly finished the box when Mum asked him to help her.

"We're decorating the baby's room, Billy," she said. "And we don't want you to feel left out."

Billy was busy, but he didn't like to say no. So he helped Mum do some painting, and quite enjoyed himself in the end.

"Can I paint my box?" he asked. Mum said he could.

In the morning, Billy was sorting out all the things in his box when his Dad said he wanted to talk to him.

Dad explained that Billy might have to go and stay at Grandma's for the night when Mum went into hospital. He said they didn't want him to feel upset or worried about it.

"I'm not," said Billy. Dad looked surprised.

But Billy liked Grandma, and when he went to visit her, she gave him a sweet.

"Can I have another one for my box?" he said. Grandma smiled.

Then one night, it happened.

Billy was woken by Mum and Dad. The baby was coming, and they had to go to the hospital. Mum and Dad did a lot of running about. Mum was smiling, but Dad looked worried.

They took Billy to Grandma's on the way, and
kissed him goodbye. Billy had his box with him.
It was ready now.

At breakfast the next morning, the phone rang.
It was Dad.

"You've got a lovely baby sister, Billy," he said.
"She looks just like you, too!"

Billy was pleased, but he didn't want to talk for
long. Dad's voice was very loud, and besides, he
wanted to show Grandma what was in his box.

Later that day, Dad came back from the hospital. He looked very tired.

"You mustn't think we won't love you any more now we've got the baby," he said, and gave Billy a big hug.

"Why would I think that?" said Billy. He was holding his box. "And when can I meet the baby?"

Dad took Billy to the hospital the next day.
Mum looked very happy.

Billy looked at his new baby sister. He smiled.

"This box is for you," he said.

"And all the things inside it are, too."

But the story doesn't end here.

Billy's baby sister

soon grew up.

She was a pain sometimes,

but Billy loved her.

And as for the box... well, Billy's sister kept that.
It turned out to be very useful...